My DADDY is Hilarious!

This book belongs to

....

For Ethan and Emily

G. P.

For Dad

C. J.

FABER & FABER has published children's books since 1929. Some of our very first publications included *Old Possum's Book of Practical Cats* by T. S. Eliot starring the now world-famous Macavity, and *The Iron Man* by Ted Hughes. Our catalogue at the time said that 'it is by reading such books that children learn the difference between the shoddy and the genuine'. We still believe in the power of reading to transform children's lives.

First published in the UK in 2020
First published in the US in 2020
by Faber and Faber Limited
Bloomsbury House, 74–77 Great Russell Street, London WC1B 3DA
Text © Gavin Puckett, 2020 Illustrations © Chris Jevons, 2020
Designed by Faber and Faber
US HB ISBN 978–0–571–33641–8
PB ISBN 978–0–571–33642–5
All rights reserved.
Printed in India

10 9 8 7 6 5 4 3 2 1

The moral rights of Gavin Puckett and Chris Jevons have been asserted.
A CIP record for this book is available from the British Library.

My DADDY is Hilarious!

Gavin Puckett

Illustrated by Chris Jevons

FABER & FABER

My daddy is the **greatest!**
My daddy is the **best!**
Daddy's lovely clothes look
so much smarter than the rest.

His aftershave smells **wonderful,**
like daffodils – it's true.
When I grow up I want to look
just like my daddy too.

Daddy's hair is shiny. It's wavy, and so sleek.
Daddy's hair is . . . **Oh!** I've spotted something odd this week . . .

His hair was brown this morning, with little bits of grey,

But now it's black and all the silver bits have gone away!

Now, it's bath time on a Friday and I've had another fright.
Dad was in the bathroom for a long, long time tonight . . .

When he appeared, my mum looked stunned – she coughed
and spluttered, **"Yikes!"**

Daddy's hair had changed again . . .

It's turned **bright pink** with **spikes!**

Now Dad has got a **Mohawk** –
it must be two feet tall!
It's scraping on the ceiling!
Oh, I don't like this at all.

That looks like **Mummy's jacket,**
and I'm sure that's **Granny's dress.**
Where did you get those boots from?

Dad, you look a mess!

Are you feeling ill today?
Your face has turned
bright green . . .

Those stripy socks
you're wearing are the
silliest I have seen.

Usually at night you wear pyjamas and old slippers,

So what on earth's the meaning of that
diver's mask and flippers?

Today Dad's hair's no longer pink – it's turned **all blond** instead.
It's gone all **tight** and **curly** – Daddy looks like **our dog, Fred!**

Granny's just arrived. *She'll* know what to do.
Gran's taking off her hat and coat . . .

She looks unusual too!

And Grandpa's now . . .

an astronaut?

Uh oh, this is bad . . .

And who's that dressed up like **a witch?**

Oh, crumpets . . . it's my **dad!**

I hope that Mum can sort things out . . .

But Mum's a ninja princess!

Oh! Yes, I get it, Daddy . . .

Phew!

It's all just **fancy dress!**

My daddy is the **greatest!**
My daddy is the **best!**
My daddy's birthday costume is
much better than the rest.

My daddy is **hilarious.**
I'm telling you, **it's true!**

And now I'm in my party clothes . . .

I look like Daddy too!